Quickie
COMEBACKS

Katy Hall and Lisa Eisenberg

SCHOLASTIC INC.
New York Toronto London Auckland Sydney

No part of this publication may be reproduced in whole or in part, or stored in a retrieval system, or transmitted in any form or by any means, electronic, mechanical, photocopying, recording, or otherwise, without written permission of the publisher. For information regarding permission, write to Scholastic Inc., 730 Broadway, New York, NY 10003.

ISBN 0-590-44998-2

12 11 10 9 8 7 6 5 4 3 2 1   2 3 4 5 6 7/9

Printed in the U.S.A.   01

First Scholastic printing, April 1992

QUICKIE COMEBACKS!

Your teacher has just asked everyone to hand in a book report. You reach into your desk and pull out your report. (Do you *really* think it was a good idea to do a book report on *101 School Jokes*?) The kid behind you peers over your shoulder, looks at your paper, and asks, "Is that your book report?"

What a stupid question! How should you handle it? Should you just say, "Yes, this is my book report"? No way! Too booooring! Should you just ignore him and hope he'll disappear? Dream on! You'll never be *that* lucky!

Face it. This situation just can't be handled with a common, ordinary reaction. What is called for is a *snappy answer*! Just what *is* a snappy answer? It's a fast and funny remark that cracks up anyone who happens to hear it. (And, if you say it loudly enough, that could be the *whole class*!)

Today's kids are constantly being blasted with stupid questions and dumb comments that require rapid, rapier-witted responses. And that's why we've written this handbook of Quickie Comebacks! Just read the book once and never again will words fail you. (Although if you use any of this stuff in class, your teacher probably *will*!)

CLASSROOM COMEBACKS

Boy: Is that your book report?
Quickie Comebacks:
- No, I'm having a piece of paper for lunch.
- Gee, it *might* be mine. It's got my name on it.
- No, it's my *dog's* book report.
- No, it's *your* book report! I stole it out of your desk before class!

Teacher: Why don't you ever listen?
Quickie Comebacks:
- My ears are too full of wax.
- Huh? What'd you say?
- I *do* listen! I just don't *understand* anything!
- Aw, did you wake me up just to ask me *that*?

Star Pupil: I'm the teacher's pet.
Quickie Comebacks:
- Yeah, I heard your teacher couldn't afford a dog!
- Pet *what*? Pet rock?
- Ah-choo! I'm allergic to animals!

Teacher: Why can't you be like Nate? He uses his head!

Quickie Comebacks:

- There's a first time for everything!
- For what? A bowling ball?
- It's the little things that count!

Teacher: Why were you shouting in the classroom?

Quickie Comebacks:
- Well, you *told us* to stop whispering.
- I'm not allowed to shout at home.

Teacher: Little Louey is so bright!
Quickie Comebacks:
- Maybe he could get a job as a flashlight!
- Yeah, he really knows watts watt!
- Maybe that's why he attracts so many moths!

Teacher: Why must you talk constantly?
Quickie Comebacks:
- I have a black belt in speaking!
- I'm exercising — my vocal chords!
- I have a lot to say!

Teacher: Were you copying the answer from your neighbor's paper?

Quickie Comebacks:

- Oh, no, sir! I was just checking to see if he had mine right!
- No, I was just admiring his nice handwriting!

Teacher: Did you pass that note?
Quickie Comebacks:
- That wasn't a note! It was my mom's shopping list.
- That was a note? I thought it was the answers to the test, and I didn't want to peek!

LUNCHROOM LAUGH LINES

When you've finished cracking up your classroom, it's time to move on to the most important activity of your day — eating! Now, as everybody knows, nothing is more likely to make you lose your lunch than having to listen to some chuckle-headed comment while you're trying to chew. Be prepared! Imagine yourself in the situations on the following pages, and take a few minutes to digest these Lunchroom Laugh Lines.

Betty: Do you want your pickle?
Veronica: Yes, it's dill-icious!

Betty: Do you want all your French fries?
Teddy: No, but they all want *me*!

Betty: Do you want your hamburger?
Freddy: Oh, is that what it is! I thought it was a UFO!
Betty: A UFO?
Freddy: Right! An Unidentified Frying Object!

Quickie Comebacks:
That wasn't me! That was:
- my hot dog barking!
- my celery's talk!
- the piano tuna!
- my meatball bouncing!
- my scream cheese sandwich!

BULLY BLASTERS

Your classroom is in stitches, and you've wiped up the lunchroom looneys with your quick-witted quips. But how will you handle that other thickheaded threat, the big-mouthed bully? Here's how — with the bombastic Bully Blasters on the following pages.

Quickie Comebacks:
- You look like a million dollars —
  green and wrinkled!
- You look like a movie star —
  Freddy Krueger!
- Does your face hurt? It's killing me!
- Come on! Halloween's over —
  take off the mask!

Bully: Hey, just how stupid do you think I am?

Quickie Comebacks:
- When you get a brainstorm, it only drizzles!
- You think the Kentucky Derby is a hat!
- The only time you've got anything on your mind is when you're wearing a hat!
- I hear your father took out termite insurance on your head!

Bully: Why don't you take a long walk off a short pier?

Quickie Comebacks:

- At least I can take a long walk. Your leash doesn't reach that far!
- 'Cause then I'd be just like you — all wet!
- Why don't you take a short jump off a long cliff?

OK, now you've conquered the classroom, collapsed the cafeteria, and butchered the bully. The next few pages contain some coaching tips to help you win your Phys Ed Pheuds!

Quickie Comebacks:
- I'm not playing. This is for real!
- At least I'm dribbling and not drooling like the rest of the team!
- I thought I signed up for basket-*weaving*!

Coach: You call *that* jogging?
Quickie Comebacks:
- Yeah, but I'd like to call it quits.
- No, I call it pure misery.
- If I didn't, would I still have to do it?

Coach: What kind of marks do you expect to get in physical education?

Quickie Comebacks:
- Probably just a whole lot of bruises!
- Underwater marks — all below C-level!
- Straight A's for AAAAAAAAAAAARG!

NEEDLE THE NURSE

Sometimes having to come up with all these Quickie Comebacks is enough to make a person sick. And when that happens, you'd better be ready! You'll have them in stitches after you bone up on these ways to Needle the Nurse!

School Nurse: Hmmm, I don't like the way you look.

Foy: Well, you don't look so hot yourself.

School Nurse: Have your eyes been checked?

Joy: No, they've always been plain brown.

School Nurse: I want to take your splinter out.

Roy: OK, but have it home by midnight.

School Nurse: Your poison ivy will be all gone by tomorrow.

Kim: Don't make rash promises!

School Nurse: How did you break your toe?

Jim: I dropped some tomatoes on it.

School Nurse: Tomatoes! How could tomatoes do that?

Jim: They were in a can!

School Nurse: Why are you here?

Slim: Because of sickness.

School Nurse: You mean you're sick?

Slim: No, I mean my teacher's sick — of me!

CLASSROOM CRACK-UPS

After you've visited the nurse, you'll probably have to go back to your classroom. Without a doubt, you'll find that, in your absence, your class has grown too comfortable. Hurry! Now's the time to review the Classroom Crack-ups on the next few pages.

Teacher: You can't sleep in my class!
Muffy: I could if you didn't talk so loud!

Teacher: Why were you late to school?
Tuffy: I passed a sign that said SCHOOL
AHEAD; SLOW DOWN.

Teacher: I wish you'd pay a little attention.
Buffy: I'm paying as little as I can!

Teacher: Well, how were the exam questions?

Girl: Oh, the questions were fine. It was the answers I had trouble with!

PERSONAL PUT-DOWNS

If you've followed our advice up to this point, by now you should have been able to declare yourself the Quickie Comeback Czar of your school. But what about your life *outside* of school? How should you deal with your friends, parents, and . . . gasp . . . brothers and sisters? Before it's too late, you'd better brush up on the following Personal Put-downs!

Quickie Comebacks:
- No, why? Is one missing?
- No, I was hiding from the lion that's loose in our house!
- No, I'm going to a Halloween party — as Terry Cloth!
- No, I've been playing water polo with my rubber duckie.

Best Friend: Are you waiting for a bus?
Quickie Comebacks:
- No, my hobby is watching cars go by.
- Oh, my gosh! You mean this isn't the airport?
- Yes, because the bus won't wait for me!
- Yeah, does that make me a busboy?
- What are you, a *bus*-y body?

Little Boy: Did you get your hair cut?
Quickie Comebacks:
- No, I got them all cut.
- No, I got my ears lowered.
- No, it must have shrunk when I washed it.

Mom: Why did you spill chocolate ice cream all over your new shirt?

Quickie Comebacks:

- Because my old one was in the wash!
- Because I didn't have any strawberry ice cream!
- Because I wanted to see if that new stain remover really worked!
- This isn't my new shirt — it's *yours*!

THE BOTTOM OF OUR MAILBAG

Lots of times kids call us up and ask, "Can we write you?" And we always say, "Sure. It's spelled y–o–u!" But even when we're that nasty, our readers still insist on sending us letters! The following pages carry some samples from the Bottom of Our Mailbag.

DEAR
    KATY+LISA,
MY DAD SAYS
    I'VE GOT
TO LOSE TEN
POUNDS. ANY
ADVICE?
        YOURS
        TRULY
HOWARD I DOITT

K+L

Dear Howie,
We've got a
great way for
you to lose ten
pounds———
Wash your socks.

        K & L

Dear Katy & Lisa,
I am so smart.
No one in my class
can keep up with me.
Don't you think that
I should skip a grade?
Or maybe two?
Signed,
Lotta Brains

Dear Ms. Brains,
You are so bright, we
had to put on our sunglasses
just to read your letter. You
are so sharp, we suspect you
comb your hair with a pen-
cil sharpener! Listen, why skip
a grade? or even two? Do
your teacher and all the rest
of the kids in your class a big
favor and just skip school
for the rest of the year!
K & L

Dear Katy + Lisa:

My sister does
nothing but argue
with me. She says I
never listen to her
side. How do I convince
her that I have an open
mind?

Sincerely,
Al's Right

Dear Ms. Right:

We believe you have an open
mind. And we bet it matches your
mouth! Just ask your
sister to listen to reason:
if you didn't have an open
mind, then how could your
brain have fallen out?

K + L

40

Dear Katy + Lisa,

I am the only normal one in my family. All of the rest of them suffer from insanity! What should I do?

your BEST FRIEND,
Ima Nutt

Dear Ima:
Tell your family to stop suffering from insanity. They might as well enjoy it! As for you, well, we noticed your family crest on your stationery. Does the fact that it's a fruitcake surrounded by a bunch of bananas tell you anything? The next time your clock says, "cuckoo! cuckoo!" we think you should listen and believe!

K + L

Dear Katy and Lisa,
I get all A's on my report card. I am the best in my class at sports. I look like a Greek god, and my family lives in a gigantic palace with a moat around it, but still......I have a problem. No one ever believes a word I say. Can you help me out?

Insincerely,
Eli Saithetime

Dear Eli:
We'd love to help you out, but only if you promise to stay out!

K & L

42

KILLER COMEBACKS

Just when you thought it was safe to go out, you find yourself surrounded by simpletons, subjecting you to idiotic inquiries. Be prepared with the following Killer Comebacks!

Quickie Comebacks:
- No, my own personal rain cloud just rained on me!
- No, I'm an escaped talking goldfish! Please don't make me get back into my bowl!
- No. My legs, arms, and feet are crying!

Boy: Oh, do you take the bus home?
Quickie Comebacks:
- Only when my limo driver has a cold.
- Yes, it's so much easier than taking my home to the bus.
- Not if the driver will drop me off at the mall.
- I do, but I could call you a cab. "You're a cab!"

Girl: Oh, did you come to see the dentist, too?

Quickie Comebacks:

- No, I came to play *Tooth or Consequences*.
- Yes, I'm on the *drill* team.
- No, I'm just *filling* in for a friend.
- No, I came to see the dentist one.

Girl: Oh, are you here to watch the movie?
Quickie Comebacks:
- No, I'm here to get a good night's sleep.
- Movie? Oh, rats! I thought this was study hall.
- No, I just like the popcorn here.

Jan: Oops! Was that your foot I stepped on?
Quickie Comebacks:
- That's OK. I've got another one.
- *Was* is right.
- Never mind. My mom always said I had two left feet.
- Must have been mine. If it had been *your* foot, you'd be screaming in pain right now!

Quickie Comebacks:

- No, I'm in a hypnotic trance, communicating with spirit voices from the Great Beyond!
- No, I just died.
- No, somebody left the window open, and my eyes froze shut!
- Huh? You'll have to repeat the question. I was so sound asleep that I didn't hear you!

Quickie Comebacks:
- Yes, because you cut it too long!
- Don't worry. It'll grow back in time for graduation — from college.
- No, I hear the billiard-ball look is in!
- What hair?

BIRTHDAY BON MOTS

Every kid dreams about his or her birthday. So how come those dreams so often turn out to be nightmares? It's all because of the dumb questions you have to put up with! Next year, be ready. Present your relatives with the Birthday Bon Mots on the next few pages.

Quickie Comebacks:
- Oh, yes! It's just perfect — for standing on to reach my brother's Nintendo game!
- It really helped me in school. Ever since I dropped it on my foot, I haven't had to take gym!

Uncle Elroy: Well, how about a little folding money for your birthday?

Quickie Comebacks:

- Gee, are you going to bend a nickle in half like you did last year?
- OK, Uncle Elroy. How big a loan do you need?

Cousin Sid: Is that your birthday cake?
Quickie Comebacks:
- No, I iced the dog.
- No, it's my new hat.
- No, it's Frosty the Snowman in disguise!

Quickie Comebacks:
- Sure, but instead of using blindfolds, let's use mouth gags!
- Sure, and after that we can have even more fun seeing who can get the most splinters in their fingers from the sun-deck railing!
- OK, but you can't play. You're so full of hot air that you'd explode if anyone stuck a pin in you!

Passerby to Sally Sue: Oh! Are you having a birthday party?

Quickie Comebacks:

- No, I have 16 brothers and sisters, all the exact same age as myself!
- No, a band of ten-year-old outlaws has taken over my home!
- No, this is Snow White's cottage, and we're the 17 dwarves!

Uncle Elroy: Are you cutting the cake now?
Quickie Comebacks:
- No, I'm going to inspect it for worms!
- No, I'm about to chop up the table for firewood!
- No, I'm *shaving* the cake now!

READY-TO-WEAR RETORTS

Look out! They're everywhere! Dumb demands! Cloddy questions! Inane inquiries! Hurry up! Waste no time reading the following Ready-To-Wear Retorts!

Girl: Is this the line for the next movie?
Quickie Comebacks:
- No, it's the line for the *last* movie. We forgot to go inside when it started!
- No, we're all standing here to keep the sidewalk from floating away!
- No, we're all fascinated by this LOST OUR LEASE sign in the window of this closed-up dime store!
- No, we're all broke, and we're hoping for some *change* in the weather!

Boy: Is that your mother?
Quickie Comebacks:
- No, I'm dating a woman 30 years older than me!
- No, she's an FBI agent who follows me everywhere!
- No, she's my bodyguard!
- No, she's my giant best friend!
- Actually, it's my dad. He has very strange taste in clothes!

Girl: Ewww, you wear glasses?
Quickie Comebacks:
- No, I'm wearing eye muffs.
- Yes. They give me X-ray vision, and I can see through your skull into the emptiness.
- No, these things are to keep my nose from falling off.
- Only if I want to see.
- Good thing *you* don't wear glasses. If you could see clearly into a mirror, you'd die laughing!

Boy: Are you raking the grass?
Quickie Comebacks:
- No, I'm taking my pet lawn tool out for a walk!
- No, I'm gathering materials for my grass skirt so I can demonstrate the hula on the front lawn!
- No, I'm making a nest for a giant sparrow!
- No, I'm getting dinner ready for our pet moose!

AUTOMATIC ANSWERS

Sometimes people ask you questions that are so dumb you don't even want to bother to answer. But don't be lazy! Students of the Quickie Comeback have a duty to respond at all times! For particularly silly questions, it behooves you to memorize the following Automatic Answers!

They say:	*You say:*
How was having the mumps?	It was *swell*!
How was the dentist?	It was *boring*!
How did it feel when you hit your finger with that hammer?	Smashing!
How did it feel when your electricity shorted out on you?	Shocking!

They say:	*You say:*
How'd you like that power failure?	I was *de*lighted!
How'd you like that airplane trip?	Most uplifting!
How'd you like it when your basement flooded?	It had a dampening effect!
Don't you think I'm cool?	Well . . . it's true, you're not so hot!

WICKED WITTICISMS

You might think that you're safe in your own home, but you're wrong! Even in the privacy of your own home, you need a full arsenal of the following Wicked Witticisms!

Quickie Comebacks:
- No, I'm watching the shelf!
- No, I'm watching a different show, but the TV is watching this one!
- No, I'm watching the commercials in between!
- No, the TV's watching me!
- I *was* watching this show till you interrupted.

Quickie Comebacks:
- No, I'm watching TV. But I'll have to admit this show *is* a little boring!
- No, I'm watching the salad dressing!
- No, I'm taking a nap. This *is* a Westing House, isn't it?
- No, I'm saluting the general — General Electric!
- No, I'm just trying to be cool!

Sister: Are you going to sit there?
Quickie Comebacks:
- No, actually, I'm trying to stand up and run away, but an army of miniature people has lassoed me and is trying to tie me to this chair!
- No, I'm going to move to a different room, but I thought I'd sit down on the chair before I carry it out of here!
- No, I'm doing a new exercise for my back. Stand up! Sit down! One, two, three! Stand up! Sit down! Break your knee!
- No, I'm trying to get the chair to start a conga line with me. Come on, rocker baby, let's boogie!

Passerby: Did you hurt yourself?
Quickie Comebacks:
- No, I'm just sitting here licking catsup off my leg!
- No, I'm just pretending to be hurt so my bike will feel sorry for me!
- No, I'm an extra in a movie. I'm made up as a zombie, recently returned from the grave!
- No, I'm painting the sidewalk red — with my *knee*!

Quickie Comebacks:

- Well, it's really only nine, but my family is ahead of its time!
- Time for *you* to get some glasses!
- Time to leave . . . for *you*!
- What'd you say? That great big clock on the wall was ticking so loudly, I couldn't hear you!

Quickie Comebacks:
- No, we're playing Throw!
- No, that tiny sphere is an alien world, and we're using our fingers to communicate with it!
- No, we keep trying to get rid of this obnoxious ball — but it keeps leaping back into our hands!
- No! What looks like a ball to you is really my pet hamster practicing her skydiving!

BACK-TO-SCHOOL COMEBACKS

You thought you'd made it out of school, didn't you? No way. Prepare yourself with the following Back-to-School Comebacks!

Slim: Are you waiting to see the principal?
Quickie Comebacks:
- No, I thought the bus stopped here.
- No, he's waiting to see me!
- Yes, but if you tell me what he looks like, then I can go back to class!
- No, I'm just sitting here because I'm tired — tired of answering stupid questions!

Slim: Are you the only one waiting to see the principal?

Quickie Comebacks:

- No! Watch out! You just stepped on my imaginary friend!
- Well, I guess so . . . except for that crazed monster about to grab the back of your neck!
- Principal? What makes you think I'm waiting to see the principal? I'm just here to hold this bench together till the secretary gets back with the glue!

Principal: Are you the child who's responsible for this?

Quickie Comebacks:
- No, but I saw the whole thing! For my safety, do you think you could get me into the Federal Witness Protection Program?
- No, I'm the new playground monitor you hired yesterday. Pretty effective disguise, right?
- No, I'm with the police. Plainclothes division. Please don't blow my cover!
- Yes, but my teacher *asked* me to do it. Just this morning he said, "Will you please give me a *break* today?!"

Quickie Comebacks:

- No, it's my history report. I'm writing about the food of ancient Egypt!
- No, it's your lunch, but I've had it since last month. Would you like it back?
- No, it's your lunch. Somehow our backpacks must have gotten mixed up and . . . oh no! You just ate my science project!
- No, it's my pet tuna sandwich. Would you like to hold it in your lap for a while?

MORE LETTERS FROM THE BOTTOM OF OUR MAILBAG

We tried to finish this book as fast as we could so we wouldn't have to answer any more of our readers' dumb questions. Unfortunately, you were just too quick for us. So, you have only yourselves to blame for More Letters from the Bottom of Our Mailbag.

Dear Katy + Lisa,
   My parents have
a cow just ⚹ because
I never want to
clean ⚹⚹ my Room.
What should I say
to them?
                  A. MESS.

Dear A,
   Why don't you offer
to mooooove out of
the house and into the
barn where it looks like
you belong?
                  Katy + Lisa

Dear Katy + Lisa,

My father's always running
around taking pictures of me, but
they just don't do my great beauty
justice. What should I tell him?

A. Donis

Dear A.
You don't need justice!
You need mercy! Why don't
you eat your father's film
and hope nothing develops?
If you're silly enough to
swallow our advice, you'll
swallow anything!
Katy + Lisa

DEAR KATY & LISA,
 I HEAR YOU TWO
CHEAPSKATES ARE NOW
CHARGING $10 TO ANSWER
A QUESTION FROM ONE OF
YOUR READERS. DON'T
YOU THINK THAT'S A
HIGH PRICE?

I. RATE

Dear I,
 Yes. That'll be
$10, please.
 Katy & Lisa

Dear Katy + Lisa,

Everyone calls me an egghead. How can I ever hope to be as cool as the two of you?

Nita Help

Dear Nita,

We are cool because we have so many fans. From your letter it sounds as if you're just too shell fish to ever be cool. All yokking aside, you must be cracked to think you could ever be as cool as we are anyway!

Katy + Lisa

RUDE ROOM REMARKS

Well, you're almost finished. You've learned how to handle dumb questions in your classroom, in the cafeteria, in the gym, in the nurse's office, at your birthday party, in your home, and in the outside world. There's just one place left — and that's in your very own room! So lock the doors and windows and get ready to read the following Rude Room Remarks!

Quickie Comebacks:
- No, I'm getting up. I've been sleeping for the last 24 hours!
- No, I'm checking under the covers to see if any of your fleas got in here!
- No, I'm going to iron my sheets with my body!
- No, I ran over Mom and Dad with a steamroller, and I'm putting their little flat bodies in here for safekeeping!

Here it is. The last Quickie Comeback to the dumbest question in the whole world!

Girl: How'd you like that book *Quickie Comebacks?*

Quickie Comebacks:
- Great! But then, of course, I just love to suffer!
- Swell . . . for a garbage-can liner!
- Well, my dog loved it. He ate the whole thing, and it didn't even make him sick!
- To tell you the truth, I really only liked one part of it, and that was on the last page where it said:

THE END!